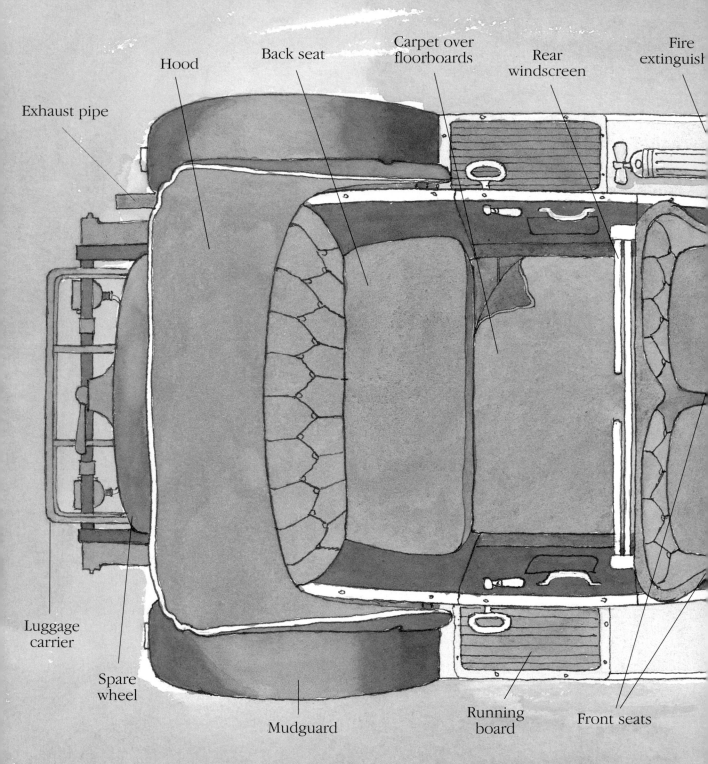

Exhaust pipe

Hood

Back seat

Carpet over
floorboards

Rear
windscreen

Fire
extinguish

Luggage
carrier

Spare
wheel

Mudguard

Running
board

Front seats

This is a bird's-eye view of GUMDROP. He is an
Austin Clifton Heavy 12/4, made in 1926. The plan
shows every detail – except the secret switches!

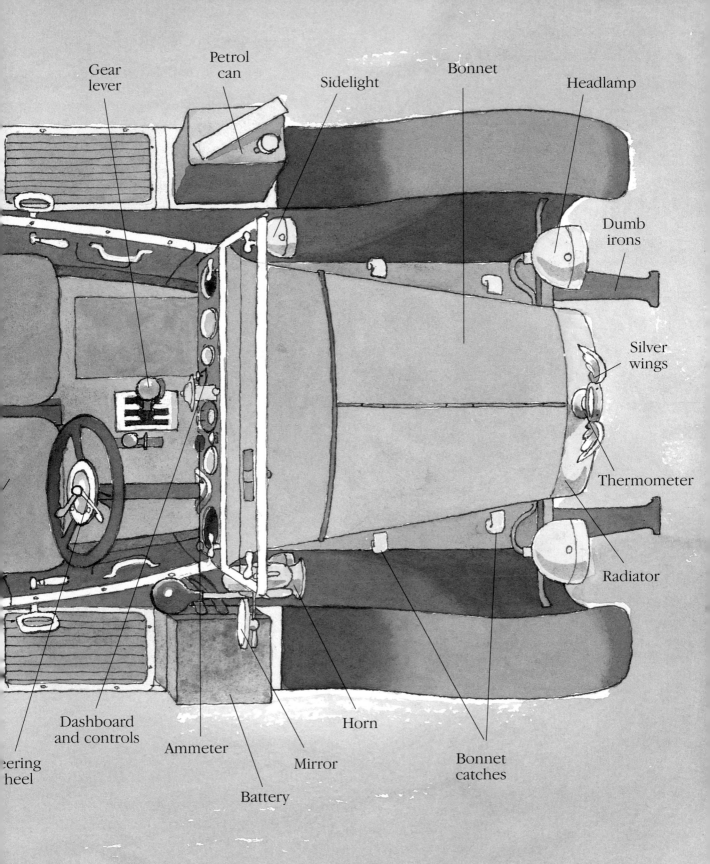

Gear
lever

Petrol
can

Sidelight

Bonnet

Headlamp

Dumb
irons

Silver
wings

Thermometer

Radiator

Dashboard
and controls

Ammeter

Horn

Mirror

Bonnet
catches

eering
heel

Battery

For Mimi,
who polished my story,
with love.

GUMDROP
and the Secret Switches

Written and illustrated by
Val Biro

AWARD PUBLICATIONS LIMITED

Mr Josiah Oldcastle had an old car called Gumdrop.
For him it was the best car in the world – except for one
thing. It wasn't fast enough to go in a race; and he
would have enjoyed racing in Gumdrop.

"Never mind," he told his dog Horace, "we can still go and just watch the other cars." Horace woofed, because he liked trips in Gumdrop.

So it was that one fine day they parked Gumdrop in a peaceful cow meadow to have their picnic. They were on their way to the Vintage Car Race, but there was time enough to relax and enjoy the warm sun.

Horace felt frisky after his snack, and began to sniff round the knobs and switches on the dashboard. One brass knob smelled so good that he took it in his mouth before Mr Oldcastle could stop him, and pulled.

Instantly the whole ammeter casing flew open as if on a hinge!

"Now look what you've done…" cried Mr Oldcastle – and stared. For behind the open casing there was a red knob which he'd never seen before; which shouldn't have been there in the first place. It looked like some sort of a switch – maybe a *secret* switch!

But what was it for? There was a label under it, sure enough, which said POTBARC. What did it mean? Mr Oldcastle had to work it out.

Could it be an acronym? Then each of these letters would be the first letters of other words. But which words? He thought for a while, then "I've got it!" he cried and jumped out to dance for joy. "**Pull Out To Beat Any Racing Car.** Gumdrop can now enter the race after all!"

And that's exactly what happened. There stood
Gumdrop among the fastest vintage cars that had ever
assembled for such a race. The other drivers looked at
Gumdrop and wondered how such a slow car could
ever stand a chance against theirs; but Mr Oldcastle,
in a crash helmet, was ready.

Horace was a little alarmed by the noise of the engines, so he hid himself under the carpet in the back. The flag went up, the horn blared out – and they were off.

The other cars thundered away in a cloud of smoke, even before Gumdrop was in top gear. But then Mr Oldcastle pulled out the secret switch. The engine began to roar like a jumbo jet, flames and smoke gushed from the exhaust pipe and Gumdrop leaped forward like a space-rocket!

In no time he caught up with the others, who were astonished – and angry – to see Gumdrop scorch past, wreathed in flames, to win the race.

The crowds cheered but the other drivers were furious. "Impossible!" they cried. "Gumdrop's a fraud! You've cheated! An absolute disgrace!"

Mr Oldcastle felt rather guilty about the secret switch, which he should have declared before the race, and apologised. To avoid more trouble he said goodbye and drove away.

But that wasn't good enough for the angry drivers; they wanted to teach him a lesson.

So they pursued Gumdrop in their cars and were catching up fast, because Mr Oldcastle found that the POTBARC switch wouldn't work a second time.

He tried to shake them off by turning into a field –
but the other drivers were getting nearer still.

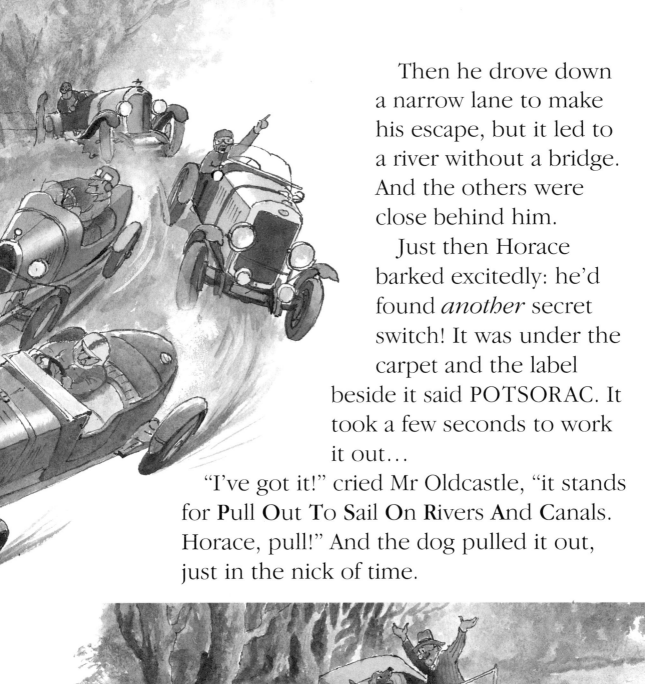

Then he drove down a narrow lane to make his escape, but it led to a river without a bridge. And the others were close behind him.

Just then Horace barked excitedly: he'd found *another* secret switch! It was under the carpet and the label beside it said POTSORAC. It took a few seconds to work it out…

"I've got it!" cried Mr Oldcastle, "it stands for **P**ull **O**ut **T**o **S**ail **O**n **R**ivers **A**nd **C**anals. Horace, pull!" And the dog pulled it out, just in the nick of time.

Gumdrop rolled forward and *splashed* into the water before the angry drivers could catch them! His big tyres acted as magic lifebelts which kept him safely afloat. Mr Oldcastle waved goodbye to the others who were left raging helplessly on the riverbank.

The chase was over (or so he thought). He could now enjoy floating gently along – they were on a canal by then – and relax after all the excitement. Horace was enjoying himself too: he stood beside the battery box looking for fish.

But their peace was soon shattered by loud voices. The angry drivers had once more caught up with them! They surrounded the canal lock and shouted, "So there you are! We'll catch you now. There's no escaping this time!"

They crowded on to the lock gates and got ready to catch Mr Oldcastle as soon as Gumdrop reached them. He sighed and was preparing himself for what was to come, when he heard Horace barking excitedly again. "What's this?" he said. "Surely not…"

Yes, it was! Horace had found a *third* secret switch, this time behind the battery box.

It had a label too that said POTFLAB. In a moment Mr Oldcastle knew what it meant.

"But of course! It is exactly what we need, because the label means **P**ull **O**ut **T**o **F**ly **L**ike **A** **B**ird!"

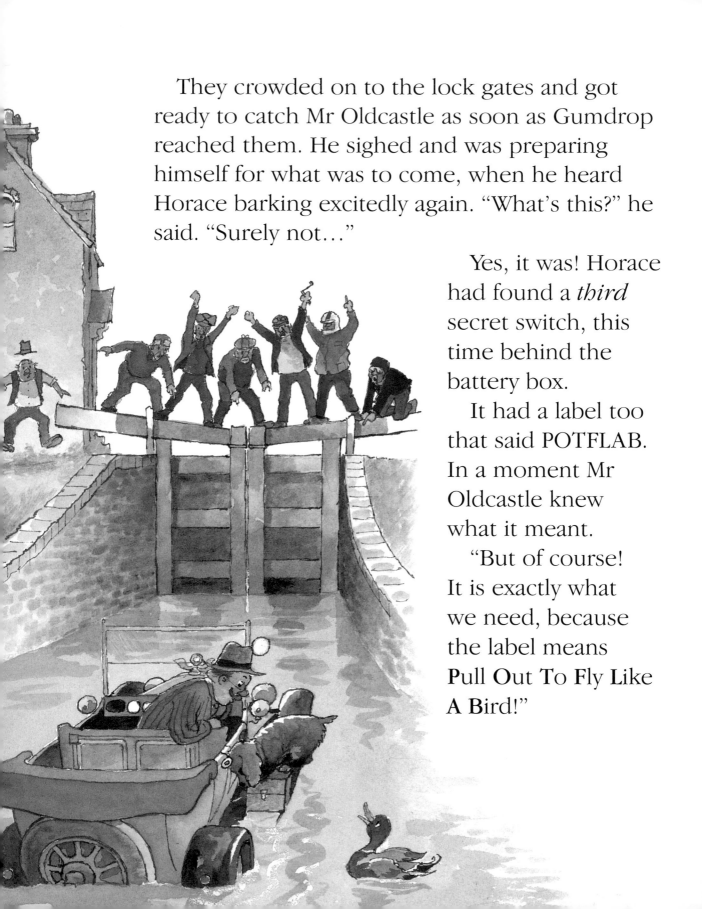

As Horace pulled the switch, the silver wings on top of the radiator began to rotate like helicopter blades, and Gumdrop rose into the air and flew in a graceful arc above the angry drivers, splashing them with water.

"That's better," said Mr Oldcastle, patting Horace for being such a clever dog.

The drivers were shaking their fists, and one fell into the water as Mr Oldcastle flew Gumdrop up into the sky.

The view up there was superb. Suddenly he heard voices behind him.

"Come and join our Vintage Flying Display," said one of the parachutists, thinking that this car must be some sort of a plane.

Mr Oldcastle would have liked to, but he didn't know how to land Gumdrop safely. Even Horace, who now sat beside him, seemed to have run out of ideas.

As Mr Oldcastle tried to work out which switch to use for landing, something happened. Something dreadful happened.

All of a sudden the engine began to cough and miss, and with a final splutter it stopped. The silver wings rotated slower and slower, until they stopped as well.

"Petrol!" cried Mr Oldcastle, "we've run out of petrol and I can't get to the can!"

There was nothing to be done this time. As Gumdrop began to glide towards earth, Mr Oldcastle folded Horace in his arms and shut his eyes.

When he opened them again, he was amazed to see that they were back in the cow meadow once more: even the picnic was where they had left it.

But how did Gumdrop manage to land so safely? Was it his dog Horace being clever again – or was the whole adventure just a dream?

At any rate they were both safe and sound, and Gumdrop was fine too. What's more, there was no sign of any secret switches anywhere. Which was just as well, thought Mr Oldcastle, because they only caused trouble.

Whether it had been a dream or not, he decided to leave the Vintage Car Race well alone this time. What if those angry drivers were real after all: then there'd be *real* trouble.

In any case, Mr Oldcastle felt that racing would have been too fast, sailing too wet and flying too dangerous for Gumdrop. He'd much rather stay firmly on the ground.

So they turned and drove home for tea.

ISBN 1-84135-331-0

Copyright © 1981 Val Biro
This edition copyright © 2004 Val Biro

First published 1981 by Hodder and Stoughton Children' Books
This revised edition first published 2004 by Award Publications Limited,
27 Longford Street, London NW1 3DZ

Printed in Malaysia